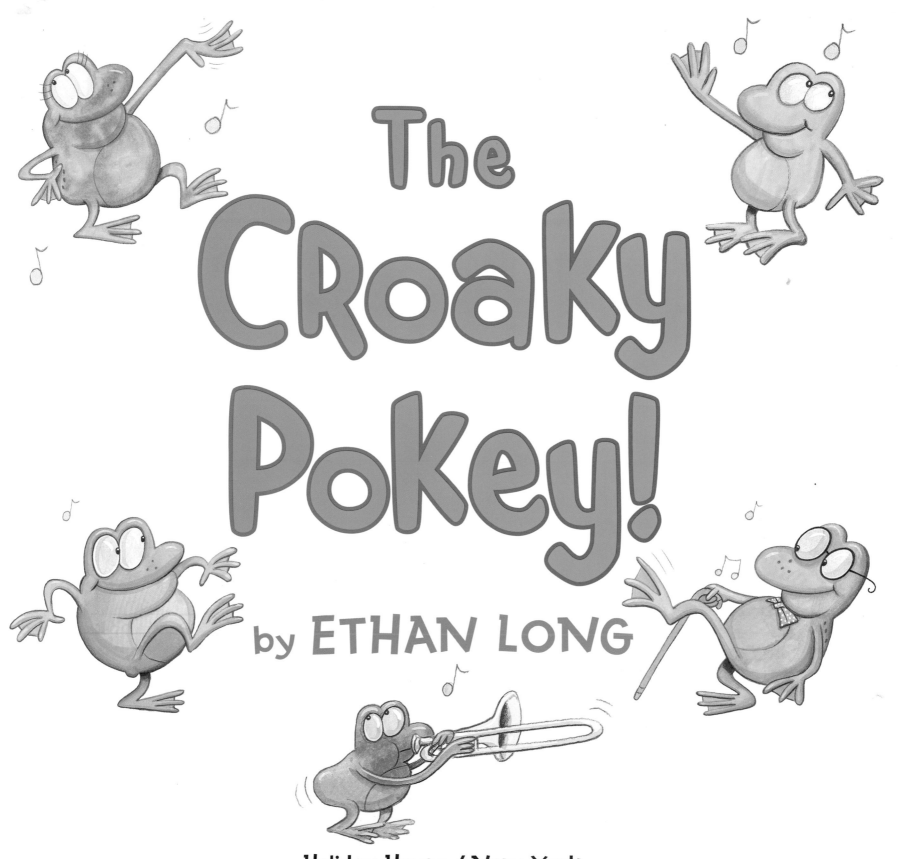

The Croaky Pokey!

by ETHAN LONG

Holiday House / New York

To my sister,
Ashley, who
grew out of her
frog collection
but, luckily, not her
sense of humor.
Love, Ethan

HOLIDAY HOUSE is registered in the U.S. Patent and Trademark Office.
Printed and bound in October 2010 at Kwong Fat Offset Co., Ltd., Dongguan City,
Quang Dong Province, China.
The text typeface is Family Dog Fat.
The illustrations for this book were created using frog saliva and bug juice,
painted with a stork feather. Actually, it was watercolor and colored pencil
on Strathmore cold press watercolor paper.
www.holidayhouse.com
First Edition
1 3 5 7 9 10 8 6 4 2
Library of Congress Cataloging-in-Publication Data
Long, Ethan.
The Croaky Pokey / by Ethan Long. — 1st ed.
p. cm.
Summary: Frogs sing and do their own version of the Hokey Pokey.
ISBN 978-0-8234-2291-3 (hardcover)
1. Children's songs—Texts. [1. Frogs—Songs and music. 2. Songs.] I. Title.
PZ8.3.L8477Cr 2011
782.42—dc22
[E]
2010023675

Ethan Long's *The Croaky Pokey!* is based on an old children's game
originally played in the British Isles. The oldest known printed
version is "Hinkum-Booby" and appeared in *Popular Rhymes
of Scotland* by R. Chamber, published in Edinburgh in 1842.
The oldest known American printed version appeared as
"Right Elbow In" in *Games and Songs of American Children*
by William Wells Newell, published in New York in 1883.
Many versions of this game are played and sung today.

Hey, everyone! Let's do the Croaky Pokey!

Put your right hand in,
Put your right hand out,
Put your right hand in,
And wave it all about,

Hop the Croaky Pokey
As we chase a fly around,
Right in the froggy's mouth!

Put your left hand in,
Put your left hand out,
Put your left hand in,
And wave it all about,

Hop the Croaky Pokey
As we chase a fly around,
Right in the froggy's mouth!

Put your right foot in,
Put your right foot out,
Put your right foot in,
And wave it all about,

Hop the Croaky Pokey
As we chase a fly around,
Right in the froggy's mouth!

Put your left foot in,
Put your left foot out,
Put your left foot in,
And wave it all about,

Hop the Croaky Pokey
As we chase a fly around,
Right in the froggy's mouth!

Put your head in,
Put your head out,
Put your head in,
And wave it all about,

Hop the Croaky Pokey
As we chase a fly around,
Right in the froggy's mouth!

Put your backside in,
Put your backside out,
Put your backside in,
And wave it all about,

Hop the Croaky Pokey
As we chase a fly around,
Right in the froggy's mouth!

Put your whole self in,
Put your whole self out,
Put your whole self in,
And wave it all about,

Hop the Croaky Pokey
As we chase a fly around . . .

SLURP!

Right in the fishy's mouth!